It's five years since Ben Tennyson last transformed into aliens and fought crime with his cousin Gwen and their Grandpa Max.

Now 15 years old, Ben is once again forced to turn to the Omnitrix to help fight a new and more sinister threat – the HighBreed, DNAliens and the Forever Knights, who team up to take over the world.

The watch-like Omnitrix has re-programmed itself and has a complete set of ten, brand new alien choices for Ben to get to grips with. Helped by his cousin Gwen with her magical powers and Ben's former enemy, Kevin E. Levin, Ben is soon all set to go hero once again!

NOW READ ON . . .

EGMONT
We bring stories to life

This edition first published in Great Britain 2010
by Egmont UK Limited
239 Kensington High Street
London W8 6SA

Adapted by Barry Hutchison

1 3 5 7 9 10 8 6 4 2

Printed and bound in Great Britain

The Forest Stewardship Council (FSC) is an international,
non-governmental organisation dedicated to promoting
responsible management of the world's forests. FSC operates
a system of forest certification and product labelling that
allows consumers to identify wood and wood-based products
from well-managed forests.

For more information about Egmont's paper buying policy,
please visit www.egmont.co.uk/ethicalpublishing
For more information about the FSC, please visit their
website at www.fsc.org

MAX OUT

CHAPTER ONE

SANTA MIRA

The rain came down in sheets, rattling like gunfire on the tin metal roof of the Cozy Cup Diner. A figure stood there in the cold, wet night, his eyes locked on the coffee shop's steamed-up window.

Icy drops of rain trickled down beneath the collar of the man's coat, making him shiver.

He pulled the coat tighter around him, adjusted the brim of his hat, and set off towards the front door of the diner.

A bell above the door gave a merry jingle as the man stepped inside. Over by the counter, a grey-haired waitress looked up at her customer. The badge on her uniform said 'Edna'. Other than the man, she was the only person in the place.

Edna's gaze followed the new arrival as he crossed to a booth and squeezed his plump frame into a seat behind the table.

A dirty menu was shoved in front of him. 'Like to hear about the special?'

'Just coffee,' the mysterious man replied.

'Don't get many strangers here,' Edna said. 'What brings you to Santa Mira?'

'Great fishing. Great weather.'

Edna looked out of the window as a flash of lightning cracked the sky. 'Our fish are all farm raised. And this is the rainy season.'

The man slipped his hat off, revealing a head of neatly cropped grey hair. Grandpa Max smiled at the waitress.

'I was misinformed,' he said.

With a shrug, Edna slipped a plate on to the table in front of him. It was covered by a grubby metal lid. 'Here's your special.'

Max glanced down at the plate. 'I didn't order that,' he said.

'It's on the house,' Edna smirked, lifting the lid off the plate.

A purple octopus-like alien sprung forwards, its teeth chomping hungrily. Max's Plumber instincts kicked in and he managed to knock the alien away. He recognised the creature as a Xenocyte – nasty critters with six legs, one eye and a brain that bulged unpleasantly on the top of their bodies.

A pair of strong arms grabbed him from behind. Max snapped his head backwards, against Edna's nose. Unharmed, the waitress didn't even flinch.

'You're one strong lady,' said Max.
'Or are you?'

Reaching behind him, Max caught hold of Edna's hair and pulled. Her skin came away in his hand, revealing the bulging, bug-eye of a DNAlien.

'DNAlien' was the nickname given to the minions of the HighBreed, an evil alien race bent on total world domination. The DNAliens had once been human, until Xenocytes had merged with them, turning their bodies into little more than mindless drones for the HighBreed to control.

Max lifted his feet and placed them against the side of the table. With a grunt he shoved backwards, sending both him and the DNAlien crashing into the table directly behind.

CRRAASH!

The DNAlien hit the tabletop first. The force of Grandpa's push made the table snap in two as the creature fell to the floor. Max rolled sideways to safety, fighting for breath. He had knocked one alien out, but he was far from out of danger.

The Xenocyte screeched as it scuttled across the floor towards him. If it managed to clamp on to his head it would begin bonding with him. Then he would be completely under the HighBreeds' control.

Grandpa reached up and snatched a heavy coffee pot from the diner counter. With a roar he brought the hot, metal container smashing down. The Xenocyte's squidgy body burst with a sickening squelch.

Another bolt of lightning flashed across the sky as Grandpa Max got shakily to his feet. He looked down at the fallen aliens and sneered. 'I said "just coffee".'

'Uh . . . no,' scowled Kevin, polishing the bonnet of his car. 'Or let me put it another way.' He glanced up at Ben. 'No.'

'Come on, Kevin, he's my cousin,' Ben pleaded. Kevin had been cleaning his car for hours, and Ben had been arguing with him almost as long. 'He was supposed to be home from college two days ago.'

'And you want me to waste my time driving around, looking for your cousin?'

'I know how it sounds,' Ben replied. 'The police said to wait. I'm sure he's fine, we just don't know where he is.'

'Daytona Beach or Fort Lauderdale,' Kevin shrugged, his attention still fixed on his car. The polished metal gleamed in the light of the full moon. 'He's a college student.'

'No. He called from the road and said his car broke down in some town called Santa Mira,' Ben told him. 'We haven't heard anything since. His folks are worried.'

'And I'm supposed to care why?'

'Because he's my brother,' said a voice from nearby. Kevin looked up and saw Gwen. Her skin was pale and her eyes were puffy, like she'd been crying. She looked scared.

Kevin sighed and straightened himself up. 'Get in.'

It was a long way to Santa Mira, and it was almost midnight by the time they turned off the main road and pulled into the town. The rain battered down so hard the car's windscreen wipers were barely able to keep up.

'You're really sweet to do this, Kevin. Ken is – '

'What?' Kevin laughed. 'Ken? Your brother's name is Ken? Gwen and Ken Tennyson? What're your folks' names, Sven and Jen?' He glanced in his rear view mirror and grinned. 'I'm talking to you, Ben.'

'Yes. Our names rhyme and you noticed,' Ben replied. 'Good for you.'

'Just having some fun, man,' said Kevin. 'I don't see what the big deal is.'

'Ken took Ben to his first soccer game,' explained Gwen, softly. 'When his band played, he snuck me and my friends backstage.' She bit her lip as she stared through the window at the rain. 'Ken's the coolest guy in the world.'

Kevin nodded towards the run-down, deserted buildings that lined the streets of Santa Mira. 'For a guy who's so cool, he sure picked a lame spot for a holiday.'

'Ken is totally cool,' Gwen said, defensively, 'and he didn't choose where the Awesome-mobile broke down.'

Kevin almost choked on his own laughter. 'The "Awesome-mobile"?'

'It's his car,' Ben explained.

'I told you, he's cool.'

'Oh, yeah,' Kevin sniggered. 'Who could doubt it?'

'I say we hit the garages in town,' Ben suggested. 'Find Ken's car, find Ken.'

'Good idea,' agreed Kevin. 'I mean, how many garages can this one horse town support, do you think?'

'Five,' Kevin groaned. 'Five garages.'

'Five garages so far,' corrected Ben. They were standing outside the fifth garage they had come across. Like the other four, it was locked up for the night. Ben had his face almost pressed against a grubby window, trying to see inside.

'And if the Awesome-mobile isn't in this one,' he said, 'we'll have to keep . . . bingo!'

Kevin pushed him out of the way, suddenly interested. 'You found a bingo game?'

'I found his car,' said Ben, pointing towards the far corner of the garage.

Narrowing his eyes, Kevin peered into the near-darkness. There, lurking in the corner, was the sorriest excuse for a car he had ever seen. Every part of it seemed to be either rusting, held in place by sticky tape, or both.

'That's the Awesome-mobile? That thing makes the Rustbucket look like a Ferrari.'

Gwen stepped back from the garage, looking around for anything that would tell them what time it would reopen the next day.

Just as she spotted the list of opening times, Kevin drove his shoulder hard against the door. There was a short, sharp snap of wood, and the door swung open.

Gwen scowled. 'Kevin!'

'Don't worry,' Kevin smiled, 'Ken is so cool he'll be happy to pay for that.'

Sneaking inside the garage, the three heroes began searching around and inside the car. Kevin wrinkled his nose in disgust when he opened a bulging grey sack that was sitting on the front seat.

'Dirty laundry for Mum to wash,' he said, half-choking. 'This guy really is a class act.'

'There must be a clue in here to help us find Ken,' Gwen said.

Ben lifted the car's bonnet. He peered down at the oil-stained engine, not sure what he was looking for.

'Whoa, what do we have here?' muttered Kevin, appearing behind Ben. He reached into the engine bay and detached a small silver object no larger than a matchbox.

'What is it?' Ben asked.

'The only thing in here not covered in rust. It's alien tech. Projects a field that dampens internal combustion.'

'His car was sabotaged?' Gwen gasped.

'Why? Ken's – '

'Too cool?'

'Too normal,' corrected Ben. 'He doesn't know anything about the aliens. Why would they go after him?'

As Kevin bent down to examine the engine more closely, Gwen leaned on the side of the car. Her hand touched something cold and slimy and she quickly pulled it away.

'Gross,' she frowned, examining the sticky yellow ooze that trickled along her fingers. 'What is this?'

'I don't know,' said Ben. He held up his watch. A bright green light was blinking furiously on its display. 'But the Omnitrix doesn't like it.'

'What's going on here?' mumbled Gwen.

A sound to their left caught their attention. All three of them spun on the spot and were surprised to find themselves facing two angry-looking men.

The larger of the two spat on the garage floor as he eyed the three heroes. 'Well now,' he said, menacingly. 'Wouldn't mind knowing that myself.'

CHAPTER TWO

SLIMEBALLS

The man was wearing mechanic's overalls and dirty gloves. Long strands of greasy hair poked out from beneath his filthy baseball cap. 'What are you lot doing in my garage?' he demanded.

The other man was carrying a large plastic cooler box. He sat it down on the ground before scurrying up to join his friend. He was dressed almost identically to the first man, but his eyes were darker and narrower.

'You want me to call the sheriff, Moe?' he asked, revealing a mouth full of rotten teeth.

Ben spotted the name tag on the man's overalls. 'Yeah, you do that, Shem,' he suggested. 'I bet they'd be real interested to find out what happened to the kid who owns this car.'

'Whaddaya mean?' drawled Moe. 'How should we know? He dropped off the car, we fixed it, he didn't come back.'

Kevin reached in through the car's window and turned the key. The engine spluttered once, made a sound like grinding metal, then died.

'You fixed it, huh?'

Unseen by any of them, Gwen had crept around behind Moe and Shem. She knelt down beside the cooler box and carefully prised open the lid. A thin layer of yellow goo lined the inside of the box.

'More slime,' she said, pulling away quickly in disgust.

'OK, that's it,' Ben snapped, approaching the mechanics. 'What is that stuff anyway? What was in there?'

Before the men could reply, a bolt of lightning lit up the night. The electrical surge made both men's skin flicker and become see-through, revealing strange and hideous alien shapes underneath.

'Check it out,' said Kevin. It's the DNA Hillbillies.'

Suddenly, Moe's throat began to swell and bulge. He opened his mouth and retched like he was about to be sick. Instead he coughed up a huge blob of yellow goo. It caught Gwen by surprise, splattering into her and pinning her against the garage wall.

Ben twisted the dial of the Omnitrix, but another ball of flying ooze swiftly encased him,

and he, too, found himself stuck to the wall like a fly to flypaper. He managed to lift his head in time to see Kevin trapped the same way.

Moe and Shem reached up and caught hold of their own faces. With a yank, the fake skin fell away, and their holographic disguises fizzled out. The two DNAliens crept closer to the helpless heroes, their pin-sharp teeth snapping hungrily at the air.

Ben struggled against the smelly yellow ooze. It had already begun to dry. In a few moments it would be rock hard and there would be no possible way to escape. His arm ached as he heaved it across his body. He gritted his teeth against the pain until his fingers at last found the cool metal surface of the Omnitrix.

'Humungousaur!' he roared, as his body began to grow and change. The dino-alien's mighty muscles ripped easily through the yellow gloop. He turned on the DNAliens, his hot breath forming clouds of steam in the cold of the garage.

Meanwhile, Gwen had also come up with an escape plan. Thin blades of pink energy swirled out from her eyes. They moved quickly along her body, slicing away the ooze and allowing her to pull herself free.

Angrily, she held up a hand and blasted one of the DNAliens with her magic. Panicked, the other creature turned to run, before realising it was heading straight for the snarling Humungousaur. Spinning on the spot, the alien darted the other way, its single green eye staring nervously over its shoulder.

KA-LANG!

The alien let out a brief shriek of pain as its head smacked against the solid steel shape of Kevin.

'That's a work-related accident. You can sue,' Kevin smirked, gazing down at the motionless form of the unconscious DNAlien.

'We got 'em,' he announced. 'Now what?'

The rain continued to fall as Ben, Gwen and Kevin climbed out of the car and studied the outside of the Cozy Cup Diner. This was the place Ken had telephoned from. The last time anyone had ever heard from him.

The coffee shop was closed. A quick sweep of the area revealed nothing to indicate Ken had ever even been there. Gwen clenched her fists in frustration.

'I thought if we retraced Ken's steps we'd find a clue,' she said. 'But there's nothing here.'

THUD.

A delivery truck parked just around the corner from the coffee shop shook, as something inside it began to move. Ben and the others approached it, cautiously.

'I wouldn't say "nothing",' replied Ben.

Bracing themselves for what they might find, Ben rolled up the back door of the truck. A DNAlien wriggled around on the floor, its hands bound by glowing energy cuffs. A rag had been wedged into the creature's mouth to keep it quiet.

The DNAlien twisted, trying to get up. As it thrashed around, it toppled over a stack of cooler boxes, spilling yellow goo all over the floor. As the slime oozed closer, the Omnitrix began to flash and bleep wildly.

Kevin reached into the truck and snatched the rag from the DNAlien's mouth. Kevin was tired, cold and wet, and he needed someone to take his anger out on. 'Start talking,' he growled.

Still watching the Omnitrix, Ben brought it closer to the slime. The green light on the watch blinked faster, and the bleeping became a high-pitched alarm.

Then, as suddenly as it had started, the Omnitrix's strange behaviour stopped. A calm electronic voice emerged from somewhere within the watch.

'Unknown DNA sample acquired.'

Ben frowned. 'That's new.'

'Ben, you want to look at this,' said Gwen. She held up the rag that Kevin had pulled from the DNAlien's mouth. It was a scrap of a very familiar Hawaiian shirt.

'This is from his favourite shirt,' Ben quickly gasped.

'Whose favourite shirt?' asked Kevin.

'Grandpa Max's,' said Gwen. A pink glow crackled across her skin. With barely a twitch she wrapped the alien in powerful tendrils of magical energy. 'Tell us who tied you up,' she barked. 'Now!'

The DNAlien yelped as Gwen's energy bonds began to tighten around it. 'Max Tennyson,' the creature groaned. 'He wanted to find some kid.'

'Where is he?' demanded Gwen.

'I don't know,' winced the trapped alien. 'He cuffed me and left me here.'

'Not him. He can take care of himself,' said Gwen. 'The kid. Where is my brother?'

The tendrils were incredibly tight around the DNAlien now. Ben could see the brain on top of its head had started to bulge, as if it were about to pop. 'Hat – hatchery,' it managed to say. 'He's at the hatchery!'

'Look, I told you, I told you,' pleaded Ken. 'I have no idea where my grandfather is. I don't know anything!'

Ken struggled against the ropes that tied him to a heavy wooden chair. He'd been pulling against the bonds for hours, but all he'd done was hurt his wrists. He was well and truly trapped. Helpless. And with a hideous creature like nothing he'd ever seen before looming over him.

'I believe you,' hissed the DNAlien.

Ken allowed himself a sigh of relief. If the creature believed him, maybe it would let him go.

'Who – who are you?' he asked, in what he hoped was a friendly way.

'I'm glad you asked, Ken,' the DNAlien replied. 'I think the best way to get to know someone is to walk a mile in their shoes.'

The alien pulled the lid from a cooler box and reached inside. A Xenocyte wriggled as it was torn free from the yellow goo. The six-legged alien thrashed around excitedly as it was brought closer to Ken's face.

'What is that?' gasped Ken, horrified.

The DNAlien's mouth pulled into something like a grin. 'My shoes.'

With a disgusting **SCHLOP** the Xenocyte clamped on to the boy's face. Ken's scream echoed around the inside of the hatchery building, and out into the dark, rainy night.

CHAPTER THREE

ASSAULT ON THE HATCHERY

Kevin turned the ignition key and the engine of his car shuddered to a stop. The high, barbed-wire fence of the hatchery lay before them. Beyond it, the hatchery itself, and hopefully, Ken.

A man-sized hole had been burned through the wire mesh, providing the perfect way into the grounds of the hatchery.

Looks like someone got here before us, thought Ben, as all three of them hurried through the narrow gap. The rain lashed against them with every step, making it hard to see. They could make out three long, thin trenches cut into the ground. All three were filled with a murky green liquid, and seemed to lead all the way into the hatchery building.

'I'm cold,' complained Kevin, rubbing his arms. 'And wet.'

Ben pointed up towards a tall tower that rose high above the rest of the complex. 'Weather machine,' he said. 'The aliens are making it cold and rainy for whatever it is they're doing.'

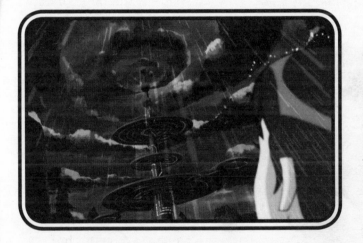

Gwen was squinting through the pouring rain, studying the main hatchery building. The entrance doors were closed. And there would almost certainly be guards standing right on the other side. They had a problem.

'How do we get in without being spotted?' she asked.

Ben thought for a moment, then peered down at one of the trenches that led into the building. It looked a bit like a long, narrow swimming pool. A long, narrow swimming pool filled to the brim with some disgusting, smelly green liquid.

Kevin guessed what was coming next. 'You gotta be kidding me,' he groaned. 'Who'd be crazy enough to swim in that?'

Deep inside the facility, a grey-haired head emerged from beneath a pool of the slimy green fluid. Grandpa Max wiped the gunk from around his eyes and studied his surroundings.

A complicated series of metal walkways

criss-crossed above him, leading to various doors dotted all around the room. Up on the left, a bulky shape leaned against a railing, its bulging green eye staring directly down at him. He'd been spotted!

The DNAlien sprinted across the walkway, its clawed hands making a grab for the button that would activate the alarm and bring reinforcements. It chattered excitedly to itself as it ran. Five metres away. Four. Three. It was going to make it!

THA-WACK!

The punch caught the alien hard on the side of the head, spinning it around just as Max let fly with another blow. This one knocked it flat on its back. The creature lay there for a moment, clutching its aching jaw. It was too dazed to react when Max pulled out the Null Void Projector gun. A beam of red energy flashed across the alien, before it was sucked into the emptiness of the Null Void.

Creeping through the closest door, Max found himself in a long, dark corridor. He ducked back around the corner before the two guards standing at the far end of the passageway could spot him.

Jamming his fingers in his mouth, Max gave a short whistle. He waited, body tensed, until he heard the clattering of the guards' footsteps racing along the corridor towards him.

Just as they drew level with the corner, Max lashed out. Two quick right hooks, a flash of the Null Projector, and both aliens were safely out of the way.

Staying alert in case of any more DNAlien activity, Max darted along the corridor. The thick metal door at the far end was electronically sealed, but it was nothing his Plumber's badge couldn't take care of. He swiped the device across the lock, and the door immediately swung open.

The glare of the lights in the room

dazzled Max as he stepped through the doorway. He blinked, adjusting to the sudden brightness, before spotting the shape lying slumped on the floor.

'Grandpa Max,' croaked the figure. 'Please help me.'

'Kenny. It's OK, boy,' said Max, reassuringly. He took Ken by the shoulder and tried to help him up. 'I'm here.'

As Ken turned, Max gave a strangled gasp of shock. A Xenocyte clung to his grandson's head, covering half his face. The one human eye Max could see seemed to plead with him as he hoisted Ken to his feet.

Suddenly, a shock of pain hit Max in the stomach. He tried to scream, but the electrical charge zapping through his body made his teeth clamp tightly together.

Max stumbled backwards. He saw the stun-gun in Ken's hand, and the grin which covered his half-alien face. And then he saw nothing but black, as he sank to the floor and slipped silently into unconsciousness.

Outside, Kevin was complaining. Again.

'Next time you ask me for a favour, remind me to say "no".'

'Don't be a baby,' snapped Gwen. 'My brother is in there, captured by DNAliens.'

They were trudging through the trench, chest-deep in the foul green liquid.

'At least he's dry,' Kevin moaned. 'And this stuff smells like – ' Something below the surface brushed against his leg, stopping him mid-sentence. 'What was that?'

All three of them scanned the surface of the water, none of them daring to make a move. The liquid rippled gently, but showed no other sign of movement.

Just before they decided it was a false alarm, a gloopy tentacle snaked up from the green fluid. In an instant it was around Gwen's neck. She barely had time to scream before it dragged her down into the murky depths of the trench.

The hatchery control centre looked like the surface of some strange alien planet. Long, stringy beams of solidified goo supported all manner of high-tech equipment. The walls, floor and ceiling were coated in a shiny red gunk. As Max was led into the room, his breath instantly formed clouds in the frosty air.

His two guards shoved him towards a raised control platform. Standing atop the platform was a towering alien, easily three metres tall. His skin was a ghostly shade of white, with four red eyes positioned just above his chest. Several more eyes covered the alien's otherwise featureless face. Max recognised the creature as a member of the HighBreed. He was probably the leader of all the DNAliens Max had encountered so far.

'Max Tennyson,' growled the HighBreed. 'You have been active in your retirement.'

Max stared up at the alien, unafraid. 'This is really just a hobby now,' he said with a shrug. 'Man my age has to stay active.'

'You have been a great irritation to us, vermin,' the HighBreed spat. 'You have delayed our plans.'

Grandpa Max nodded towards a stack of nearby cooler boxes. 'It's obvious you're producing these Xenocytes here,' he said.

'And that they somehow transform humans into these ugly freaks.'

'It can't be helped,' the alien replied. 'Their human half makes them repulsive.'

'All I want to know is why?'

'You will soon see for yourself, insect,' gloated the HighBreed. 'We are only a few hours away from completing the most crucial stage of the plan.'

'But why my grandson?' demanded Max. 'Why change Ken?'

'He was brought here as bait.' The HighBreed leaned down so his face was next to his prisoner's. 'With you out of the way, there is no one who can stop us!'

CHAPTER FOUR

INTO THE UNKNOWN

Ben's lungs burned as he lifted his head above the surface and gasped in some air. Kevin's head splashed up behind him, panic blazing behind his eyes.

'Where is she?' cried Ben.

'I can't see a thing down there!'

They ducked down below the surface, flailing their arms out, searching for any sign of Gwen. Precious seconds flowed by, until they couldn't hold their breath any longer.

They bobbed up and both gulped down a lungful of oxygen.

'Keep trying,' yelled Ben, but before they could dive again a pink glow lit up the water.

WHOOSH!

The glow exploded upwards, sending dozens of Xenocytes spiralling into the night sky. Gwen emerged from below the rippling surface. On either side of the trenches, Xenocytes plummeted to the ground with a series of slimy splats.

'Disgusting.' Gwen shuddered.

'It's about to get much worse,' warned Ben. He pointed to where the liquid flowed inside the hatchery building. The gap was narrow, and they would have to swim a long distance underwater to get to it.

Kevin shook his head. 'Oh, you're not saying – ' He watched Ben and Gwen take a breath and dive below the surface. Kevin sighed. 'Proving my point about this being the worst road trip ever!'

The trench became gradually deeper as it entered the main part of the complex. Although the water was dark and murky, Ben could make out the squirming shapes of hundreds of Xenocytes on the floor below. They crawled from inside large round pods, which Ben guessed must be eggs. They were horrible things, and Ben couldn't get past them quickly enough. He kicked his legs harder and pushed for the surface.

They emerged in the same room where Grandpa Max had popped up. Above them were the metal walkways. This time, though, there wasn't one alien standing on guard, there were dozens! The creatures snarled and spat, their eyes fixed on the intruders.

'We are not stealthy,' Ben muttered.

Kevin cracked his knuckles. 'But we kick much butt.'

On cue, Ben punched the dial of the Omnitrix. In a flash of glowing green, he transformed into a spindly blue alien, wearing what looked like a tattered robe. The robe unfolded, revealing itself to be a pair of huge, moth-like wings.

'Big Chill!' hissed the alien hero, as Gwen and Kevin both leapt from the pool.

Kevin paused to absorb the strength of the iron walkway, turning his body into living metal. He kicked out wildly, catching one DNAlien in the stomach, and sending him spinning into another gang of the hideous creatures. The whole group toppled to the ground like skittles.

Big Chill swooped down. He flew straight through five of the DNAliens, one at a time, passing through them as if he was a ghost. As he phased in and out of them, each alien found itself frozen solid and completely unable to move.

'I thought you guys liked it cold,' laughed Big Chill.

Gwen was blasting her way through another group of the creatures. Her power blasts took care of four, five, six of the aliens, slamming into them and forcing them to their knees.

A seventh alien lunged at her, but she was too fast. A bolt of pink energy crackled from her fingertips and struck the creature on the chest. As it fell, she realised there was something different about this alien. Something strangely familiar . . .

From nowhere, Kevin made a dive for the DNAlien, his fists raised. Just before he could deliver the knock-out blow, an energy shield forced him back.

'Wait!' cried Gwen. 'Get back. Get away from him!'

Freezing the last of the remaining aliens, Big Chill glided down on to the walkway beside Kevin. He gasped as the DNAlien lifted his head to reveal a partially human face.

'It's Ken,' Gwen said. 'It's my brother.'

Green light swept across Big Chill, changing him back into Ben. He studied the DNAlien's face, barely able to believe what he was seeing.

'You're right,' he nodded. 'It is Ken.'

'That's Ken?' snorted Kevin, looking down at the twisted form of the half-human, half-alien. 'He's actually less cool than his car.'

'We've got to help him,' insisted Gwen.

'He was fighting us,' Ben reminded her. 'Whatever they did to him affected his mind.'

Ken touched the Xenocyte that was

covering most of his face. A tear rolled down from his one human eye. 'What this did to m-me,' he began, before his voice grew deeper and his face darkened, 'is set me free!'

Snarling, Ken snatched up the fallen body of another DNAlien. He roared as he hurled the lifeless alien towards Ben. Dodging to the side, Ben raised his fists. He didn't want to fight Ken, but he would if he had to.

'Let's get him,' cried Kevin.

'No, don't hurt him,' pleaded Gwen. 'He's just sick.'

Ken shrieked with rage as his sister wrapped him in energy tendrils, holding him in place. 'It's that thing on him. It's making him do this.'

Kevin pushed forward and took hold of the wriggling Xenocyte. 'Then let's get it off him.' Gritting his teeth, he pulled the creature. A scream of pain burst from Ken's lips.

'Kevin, wait,' Ben yelped, pulling Kevin away. 'You're hurting him!'

As Ben drew close to Ken, the Omnitrix began to flash a worrying shade of red.

'Severe genetic damage detected,' chimed a voice from inside the watch.

Cautiously, Ben lifted the device nearer his mouth. 'Hello?' he whispered. 'Uh, Omnitrix, is that you?'

'Genetic code splicing error,' continued the watch. 'Should we attempt to repair?'

Ben glanced at his half-alien cousin. 'Try to fix Ken? Yeah. Let's do it!'

Placing his hand on the writhing Xenocyte, Ben felt a buzz of energy spread out from inside the Omnitrix. It seemed to pass through him and into the alien parasite.

'What are you doing?' asked his worried cousin, Gwen.

Ben shrugged. 'I'm not entirely sure.'

Two of the Xenocyte's tentacles thrashed up and attached themselves to Ben's face. He screwed his eyes tightly closed as they slithered across his cheeks and probed at his nostrils.

When Ben opened his eyes he almost cried out in shock. He was no longer in the hatchery. Instead he was floating down a long tunnel. The walls glowed a familiar shade of green, and he realised at once where he was.

Whoa. I'm inside the Omnitrix, he thought. A giant image of Ken's head floated along the tunnel, the Xenocyte still wrapped around it. And so was the creepy-crawly.

Ben floated onwards until he was level with the bug-alien's bulging green eye. He dug his fingers into the creature's gooey flesh and pulled. It was horrible, but he had to save Ken. He was going to save Ken.

With a soft, gloopy **SCHLOP**, hundreds of smaller tentacles began to grow from the Xenocyte's skin. They twisted and curled up Ben's arms. They wrapped around his body, around his neck, around his head.

Ben tried to scream for help, but it was too late. The tentacles cocooned him completely, and he found himself suffocating in cold, black darkness.

CHAPTER FIVE

FACING THE HIGHBREED

Ben opened his eyes. He was standing in the hatchery, Gwen and Kevin by his side. Something cold and wet was in his hand, and he realised he was holding the limp body of the Xenocyte.

Ken was on his hands and knees on the floor, groaning. The alien was no longer attached to him. He was human once more.

Ben dropped the creature and examined the Omnitrix. 'I'm going to have to get a manual for this thing,' he muttered. He smiled at his cousin. 'It's OK, Ken. Everything's going to be just fine.'

'Nothing's fine,' Ken wheezed. 'I captured Grandpa. Handed him over to them. I-I couldn't stop. It was like I was watching someone else doing it.'

'They have Grandpa Max?' Ben quizzed.

'That's why they took me. They knew he'd come for me.'

Ben glanced around at the others. 'Let's go get him.'

Ken gritted his teeth and pulled himself up. His legs wobbled, but he refused to fall. 'I'm coming with you,' he announced.

'You want to help?' asked Kevin, impressed by Ken's determination. 'Cool.'

On the floor of the control room, Max raised his head. The door was sliding open, and he had no idea what might come through. His arms and legs were tied. There would be nothing he could do to defend himself.

His face folded into a smile of relief when

he saw who stepped through the door.

'Ben!'

'Grandpa Max,' Ben replied, rushing over
to untie his grandfather's bonds.

'You're a sight for sore eyes,' Max told
him. He stood up as the ropes fell away, just in
time for Gwen to trap him in a hug.

'I'm so glad you're OK,' she whispered.

Max smiled. 'Me too, honey.' The old man
turned and faced Gwen's brother. 'Kenny.'

'Grandpa. I didn't know what I was doing,' Ken sobbed. 'I . . . I . . .'

Max's strong arms slipped around the boy's shoulders, pulling him into a warm bear-hug. 'It's OK,' he said, softly.

Grandpa Max turned to his other grandson. 'I always knew you could do it, Ben,' he smiled. 'I'm so proud of you. All of you.' Max nodded over to Kevin, who was standing a little away from the others. 'You too, Kevin. I've been watching. You've come a long way. Might even earn that Plumber's badge you swiped.'

Suddenly, a crackly voice boomed out from the control room's speaker systems.

'Attention all personnel,' announced the voice of the HighBreed, 'initiate Project DNA now.'

With a series of clanks and whirrs, the entire hatchery building seemed to come to life. Ben and the others raced to a window, where they saw long floating vehicles vacuuming

Xenocyte eggs up from the liquid-filled trenches. The egg-carriers then continued on to where hundreds of DNAliens were waiting to load the eggs on to trucks.

'What are they doing?' whispered Ben.

'They're shipping those things somewhere,' Grandpa told him. 'Putting together a DNAlien army.' Max spun to face his grandson. His expression was deadly serious. 'Stop them, Ben. These Xenocytes must be destroyed. Go.'

With a nod, Ben sprinted for the door,

Kevin, Gwen and Ken following hot on his heels.
Just before he left the control room, however,
Ben stopped and looked back at his grandfather.
'What are you going to do?'

Max smiled, but it was a thin, sad smile.
'What I have to.'

KRAKKA-WHOOSH!

The first of the trucks went up in a blinding
fireball, sparked by Gwen's power blasts. All
around the complex, DNAliens stopped their
egg-loading and swarmed to launch an attack.

Ben activated the Omnitrix, and leapt into
the air as the swirling green energy wrapped
around him, transforming him into Jet Ray. The
flying alien gained height, then sharply banked
down over the remaining trucks, zapping them
with his neuroshock lasers.

BOOM!
BOOM!
BOOM!

Fuel tanks ignited one by one, destroying most of the vehicles and the terrible cargo inside them.

Absorbing the metal of a crowbar Ken had picked up, Kevin set to work battling the DNAliens. He punched and kicked furiously, sending the creatures flailing in all directions.

Meanwhile, Ken was putting the crowbar to work. He dodged and darted around the DNAliens, stopping only to smash any Xenocyte eggs he found. He would make sure they couldn't do to anyone else what they had done to him.

Several more DNAliens closed in on Gwen. Their claws swiped at her and their teeth snapped hungrily together. Gwen floated above them, pink energy buzzing behind her eyes.

'You kidnapped my brother. Turned him into a monster. Captured my grandfather.' Gwen's fingertips lit up like fireworks. 'I have had it with you!'

A ripple of energy exploded from inside her. It hit the approaching aliens like a shockwave, knocking them out and destroying the last few remaining trucks.

Jet Ray landed on the ground beside Kevin. In the blink of an eye he was Ben again. He watched his cousin, impressed.

'Wow,' he said.

Kevin nodded. 'Yeah.'

On the building behind them, a window was lit up by a series of blinding white flashes. Ben turned and ran towards the front door. The trucks may have been stopped, but Grandpa Max was still in danger.

Ben and the others hurried through the control room. Machinery lay smashed and scattered everywhere. Grandpa had been busy.

They pushed on through the door at the back of the room, then skidded to a stop. In the centre of the cavern-like room they had entered was a mountain of eggs. There must have been thousands of them – millions, maybe. Above the mound, a weird, insect-like alien laid another egg on to the pile every few seconds.

'So, was I right?' whispered Kevin.

Ben nodded, grimly. 'Yeah. Worst road trip ever.'

A frantic struggle over to his left caught Ben's attention. He looked over to see Max battling with the HighBreed. His Grandpa was using all his strength and skill, but the alien was easily fending him off.

With a screech of triumph, the HighBreed reached out and snatched Max up with one hand. His long, black fingers tightened around

Grandpa's helpless body.

'Stay back,' hissed the HighBreed, 'or this one breathes no more.'

'Give it up, we've beaten you,' Ben shouted. 'Your factory's toast, your trucks are smashed. It's over.'

'Fools!' cackled the alien. 'More trucks can be here in a matter of hours. And my DNAlien hordes . . .' He gestured for them to look out of the window. A sea of DNAliens stood outside the building, surrounding it completely.

'Are already here,' Ben croaked.

'It ends now,' the HighBreed told him.

'Nowhere left to run.'

A grim smile spread across Grandpa Max's face. 'I wasn't running, chief. I was looking for the egg-machine.'

Max twisted his arm and reached into his pocket. The Null Void Projector glowed red as he held it up for the alien to see.

'A Null Void Projector. You think you can imprison us all?' snorted the HighBreed.

'No,' Grandpa Max admitted. He snapped the red cover off the weapon. 'But without the focusing lens, this thing'll do a pretty good imitation of a hand grenade. I figure it'll take out half a mile.'

The HighBreed hesitated. 'You wouldn't dare. You'd be destroyed. And your offspring.'

'Gwen,' Max called, 'throw up an energy shield around you and the boys and hold on tight.' He gave her an encouraging smile. 'And be a good girl.'

'Grandpa Max, no,' begged Ben, realising

what was about to happen. 'Please!'

'Sorry, Ben. It's the only way to make sure they can't do to the rest of the world what they did to Ken. You'll have to take it from here. I know you can do it. I believe in you. All of you.'

Ben tried to run forwards, but Kevin caught him by his shirt. A shimmering energy shield flew up around them, just as Max's finger pressed down on the trigger. The explosion tore through the complex; a burst of pure white energy that vapourised everything in its path.

When the smoke cleared, the energy bubble was the only thing left standing for miles around. The hatchery, the HighBreed, even the army of DNAliens were all gone.

And so was Grandpa Max.

'Whoa,' Kevin croaked. 'That was pretty hardcore.'

The energy shield fizzled out, as tears began to roll down Gwen's cheeks. 'He . . . he saved the whole world,' she sobbed.

'Yeah, he did. For now,' said Ben, his voice shaking. 'But those things aren't going to give up. It's up to someone to protect this planet.' Ben looked up at the dark night sky. It had stopped raining, but he knew the storm would not be far away. 'And like it or not, I think it's up to us!'